MAPLE RIDGE

THE NEW KID

By Grace Gilmore
Illustrated by Petra Brown

LITTLE SIMON

NEW YORK   LONDON   TORONTO   SYDNEY   NEW DELHI

This book is a work of fiction. Any references to historical events, real people, or real places are used fictitiously. Other names, characters, places, and events are products of the author's imagination, and any resemblance to actual events or places or persons, living or dead, is entirely coincidental.

LITTLE SIMON
An imprint of Simon & Schuster Children's Publishing Division
1230 Avenue of the Americas, New York, New York 10020
This Little Simon edition April 2016
Copyright © 2016 by Simon & Schuster, Inc.
All rights reserved, including the right of reproduction in whole or in part in any form.
LITTLE SIMON is a registered trademark of Simon & Schuster, Inc., and associated colophon is a trademark of Simon & Schuster, Inc.
For information about special discounts for bulk purchases, please contact Simon & Schuster Special Sales at 1-866-506-1949 or business@simonandschuster.com.
The Simon & Schuster Speakers Bureau can bring authors to your live event. For more information or to book an event, contact the Simon & Schuster Speakers Bureau at 1-866-248-3049 or visit our website at www.simonspeakers.com.
Designed by Chani Yammer
The illustrations for this book were rendered in pen and ink.
The text of this book was set in Caecilia.
Manufactured in the United States of America 0316 FFG
10 9 8 7 6 5 4 3 2 1
This book has been cataloged with the Library of Congress.
ISBN 978-1-4814-4747-8 (hc)
ISBN 978-1-4814-4746-1 (pbk)
ISBN 978-1-4814-4748-5 (eBook)

CONTENTS

CHAPTER 1

• LIBRARY DAY •

Logan Pryce yawned as he started up the hill toward the Maple Ridge School. "I'm too tired for learning today!" he complained. He had woken up before dawn to help Pa chop wood.

"But it's Wednesday!" his sister Tess said happily. She did a twirl, which made her brown braids fly.

"What's so special about Wednesdays?" their brother Drew piped up. "I like Fridays better. That's when we have our spelldowns, and I always win."

Logan rolled his eyes. At eleven, Drew was the oldest of the Pryce children. He could be a big show-off sometimes.

"Remember? Miss Ashley said that starting today, Wednesdays would be Library Day," said Tess. "We each get to pick a book to take home for a whole week!"

Tess loved to read more than just about anything. Logan thought reading was okay, although he liked inventing things a lot more.

"I helped Miss Ashley shelve the library books. I know what I'm choosing first," Tess declared.

"Little Women?" guessed Logan. "Treasure Island?"

Tess shook her head. "I've already read those. No, my first library book shall be *Birds of North America*."

"Who cares about a bunch of dumb birds?" Drew teased her.

"I do!" Tess snapped. "Birds are very interesting. For example, did you know that hummingbirds can fly backward? And that the turkey got its name because people thought it came from the country of Turkey? And ..."

Tess was still chattering about birds when the three of them reached the crest of the hill. She could be shy at times, but not when it came to things she cared about, like books and birds.

Drew leaned over to Logan. "If I have to hear any more about birds, I'm going to stick my head in the ground like an ostrich," he joked.

"Or you could flap your arms like a goose and fly away!" Logan joked back.

The two brothers chuckled. Up ahead was their one-room schoolhouse. A thin column of

smoke rose from the chimney.
The trees in the yard were
cloaked with red and yellow
leaves.

Logan spotted Kyle Chambers and Lenny Watts strolling through the door with their lunch pails. And then he spotted a boy he didn't recognize. The boy was as tall and skinny as a beanpole. He wore oval-shaped, gold-rimmed glasses and an odd hat decorated with a feather.

Exactly twenty students attended the Maple Ridge School, and Logan knew every single one.

Except for this boy. Who was he?

CHAPTER 2

● OSWALD ROBBINS ●

Inside the schoolhouse, Tess caught up to Greta Kranz and Nellie Shaw. The three of them had become friends recently.

Logan hung his hat on a hook. Then he felt someone tap him on the shoulder.

It was his best pal, Anthony Bruna. "*Pssst!* Who's the new kid?"

Anthony whispered. He pointed to the boy with the feathered hat and glasses.

"I'm not sure," replied Logan. "Doesn't he know boys aren't allowed to wear hats inside? And why is he sitting *there*?"

At school, the
boys sat on one
side of the room
and the girls sat
on the other.
The youngest
students sat
up front near
Miss Ashley,
the teacher. The
oldest students,
like Drew, Kyle,

and Lenny, sat in back. Logan and Anthony, who were eight, and Tess, who was nine, sat in the middle section.

The new kid was sitting on the girls' side, way in the back.

"Maybe we should tell him," said Anthony.

"Maybe," agreed Logan.

But before they could speak to him, Miss Ashley called everyone to attention. "Good morning, class. Please take your seats! I have two very special announcements to make before roll call."

Logan, Anthony, and all the other students hurried to their desks.

"First of all, today is our very first Library Day!" said Miss Ashley. "As you may know, some towns have free public libraries now. But since Maple Ridge does not have one yet, Mr. Bird was kind enough to donate one hundred books so our school could start its very own library."

Miss Ashley nodded toward the three brand-new shelves filled with books. Logan's jaw dropped. He had never seen that many books, not even at the general store! Logan liked Mr. Bird, who had once paid him a dollar for one of the projects from his Fix-It Shop.

"Second, I want to introduce Oswald Robbins. His family just moved here from Chicago," Miss Ashley went on.

Logan turned. It was the new kid! Oswald's face flushed beet red as everyone stared at him. He slouched down in his chair, which made his long, skinny legs look extra long and skinny. Then he mumbled something under his breath.

"Could you please speak a little louder, Oswald? We can't hear you," said Miss Ashley.

"I said to please call me Wally," he squeaked.

This time, the whole class heard. Lots of people snickered.

Miss Ashley clapped her hands. "Boys and girls! Silence! Let us make Wally feel welcome. In fact, I think we should invite him to be the first one to choose a book from our new library."

Tess raised her eyebrows.

"Go ahead, Wally. Please select a book. Also, why don't we move you to that empty desk in front of Logan Pryce?" Miss Ashley suggested.

Wally scooped up his belongings and slinked toward the library shelves. His movements reminded Logan of a weasel he once saw in Pa's cornfield.

At the shelf, Wally pushed his glasses up his nose and scanned the titles, A to Z. After a moment, he took a book from the B section. He tucked it under his arm and shuffled back to the empty desk.

Tess caught Logan's eye and frowned at Wally's book.

Logan read the title. It was *Birds of North America*—the book Tess had wanted!

CHAPTER 3

•THE ODD BOY OUT•

At recess, Logan and Anthony kicked a ball around on the grassy lawn. Nearby, a group of kids joined hands and sang "Ring around the Rosy." Still other kids jumped rope or walked on wooden stilts.

"What library book did you choose?" Logan asked as he kicked the ball to Anthony.

"*The Merry Adventures of Robin Hood,*" Anthony replied. "What about you?"

"I wasn't sure at first. Then Miss Ashley told me I would like this book called *Hans Brinker* something. It's about a brother and sister who want to enter an ice-skating contest. They don't have proper steel skates, though. Just a pair of old wooden ones." Logan grinned. "That reminds me! Did I tell you about my latest invention?"

"Gosh, no. What is it?" asked Anthony.

"Wonder Walkers!" Logan said proudly. "You know how parents get upset when you track mud into the house? Well, Wonder Walkers solve that problem. You walk on top of them, like stilts, so your shoes don't get muddy."

"That sounds swell. Can you make me a pair too?"

"Sure thing! I'm still working on the design, though."

Greta marched up to the boys. Tess and Nellie followed at her heels. "We discussed it, and we decided that it's an outrage!" Greta declared.

"Does that mean she's mad?" Anthony murmured to Logan.

Logan shrugged. "I guess."

"Of course I'm mad! We all are because poor Tess will have to wait a whole week to read *Birds of North America*," Greta huffed.

"That Wally kid had no right to take Tess's book!" Nellie chimed in.

Tess nodded, but she didn't say anything.

"How was Wally supposed to know Tess wanted that book?" asked Logan.

Greta put her hands on her hips. "He should have known, is all."

"Aw, I'm sure he

didn't mean it. He's probably a real nice kid," said Anthony.

"Hardly," Nellie scoffed.

"He's *odd*," Greta added. "Look!"

Everyone looked. Wally was sitting under a tree, munching on an apple and reading *Birds of North America*.

Wally glanced up. Logan waved, just to be friendly. So did Anthony.

But Wally didn't wave back. Instead, he sprang to his feet and ran away.

"See? He's *odd*," Greta repeated.

Logan was beginning to wonder if maybe Greta was right.

CHAPTER 4

• INTO THE WOODS •

After school, Logan invited Anthony over to his house.

"I've discovered a new shortcut!" Logan announced as they started down the road.

"That's swell! Where is it?" asked Anthony.

Logan paused to pick up a stick. He sketched out a route in the dirt.

"See here? If we take this shortcut through the woods, we'd get there a lot faster."

"Onward, then!"

"Onward!"

They continued down the road. Goldenrod and switchgrass swayed in the cool breeze. Squirrels scurried about with acorns.

"I was thinking," Anthony said to Logan. "Why do you suppose Wally's family moved here from Chicago?"

"Why wouldn't they? Maple Ridge is as fine a place to live as anywhere!" replied Logan.

"But there are no jobs here," Anthony reminded him. "Folks are *leaving* Maple Ridge so they can find work in the big cities, not the other way around."

Logan thought about this. Anthony was right. Pa had given up farming because he couldn't make enough money. Other farmers in Maple Ridge had done the same. These days, Pa worked at a glass factory in Sherman, which was two hours away by horse and buggy. Anthony's pa, Mr. Bruna, also worked in Sherman.

So what was Wally's family doing in Maple Ridge?

Logan and Anthony soon reached the edge of the woods.

"There!" Logan pointed to a neat pile of stones on the ground. "I left a marker where the path begins so I could find it again."

"That's smart!" said Anthony.

Fallen brown leaves made a crunching sound as the friends walked down the path. Logan began to chant:

"There were two blackbirds
Sat upon a hill"

Anthony joined in:

"The one was nam'd Jack
The other nam'd Gill
Fly away, Jack
Fly away, Gill
Come again, Jack
Come again, Gill"

Up ahead, a large shadow darted across the path.

Logan and Anthony stopped in their tracks.

"What . . . was . . . that?" Logan whispered.

"Gosh, I'm not sure," Anthony whispered back.

A moment later, the shadow darted across the path again. That's when Logan noticed the glasses and feathered hat.

"It's Wally Robbins!" Logan said, relieved.

Anthony's eyes grew wide. "It sure is! What's he doing here?"

The two boys crept closer. Wally ducked behind a maple tree. He held a book open in his hands as he peered this way and that.

"He could be a spy," Anthony guessed. "Maybe he's on a secret mission."

"Maybe. That would explain what he's doing in Maple Ridge," Logan agreed.

Snap!

Logan had stepped on a big, crackly branch. The loud noise made Wally spin around.

"Ahoy!" Logan called out. He didn't know what else to say.

"Ahoy!" echoed Anthony.

Wally didn't reply. Instead, he tucked his book under his arm and disappeared into the woods.

CHAPTER 5

• WONDER WALKERS •

Over the following week, the new kid known as Wally Robbins grew even more mysterious.

At school, Wally continued to keep to himself. In class, he mostly stared out the window and sketched in a leather notebook. At lunch, he ate alone. At recess, he didn't play games with the other kids; instead, he read *Birds of North America* or wandered through the woods.

The other students made fun of him, especially Kyle and Lenny, who had declared Wally the weirdest kid in all of Maple Ridge. Even kindhearted Tess had decided she was against him.

Logan thought about all this one evening as he sat in his Fix-It Shop, finishing up his first pair of Wonder Walkers. The Fix-It Shop was in the corner of the Pryces' barn, which was also home to Lightning, Miss Moo, and the other farm animals.

The Wonder Walkers were two upside-down tin cans with long pieces of twine to hold on to, like with stilts. Logan planned to bring them to school tomorrow to show Anthony during recess.

As Logan worked, he wondered: Who was Wally Robbins? Why did he avoid everyone?

Also, what was inside his leather notebook? Could it be secret spy stuff? But what was there to spy on in Maple Ridge?

After nearly a week, Logan still had no answers. Every time he tried to speak to Wally, the other boy skittered away like a nervous bird.

Over supper that night, Logan told his parents about Wally.

"He won't talk to anyone. No one likes him," Logan finished.

Drew shrugged. "He's odd, is all."

"And he steals other people's books," Tess added.

"He *didn't* steal your book!" Logan cried out.

"But Greta and Nellie *said* he did!" Tess insisted.

Logan's dog, Skeeter, got up from his spot in front of the cookstove and barked. He didn't like it when the humans in the house raised their voices.

Pa held up his hands. "Hush now, Skeeter. Children, we must be kind. It's not easy being the new person at school."

"I have a fine idea! Why don't I make a special welcome treat for Wally and bring it to your school tomorrow?" Ma suggested.

"Can Mrs. Wigglesworth and I come with you?" Annie piped up. At four years old, Annie was the youngest Pryce. Mrs. Wigglesworth was a doll that Ma had sewn for her.

Ma smiled. "Yes, Annie. In fact, you may help me bake the special treat in the morning."

"Can it please be shortbread cookies, Ma?" Logan begged.

"If you and Tess will churn some extra butter for me," replied Ma.

"Hooray, we're having shortbread cookies tomorrow!" Logan shouted.

"Hooray! And tomorrow is Library Day!" Tess shouted. "I'll finally get to read *Birds of North America*."

Skeeter barked again. Logan grinned and dug into his squash soup. Tomorrow promised to be a very good day!

CHAPTER 6

• MA'S SPECIAL • TREAT

It was raining on Wednesday morning, so Ma drove Logan, Tess, and Drew to the schoolhouse in the buggy. Pa caught a ride to Sherman with Anthony's father.

Annie squeezed between Logan and Tess in back. "We're going to school, Mrs. Wigglesworth!" she told her doll.

"You'll be going to school for real in a few years, Annie. Won't that be so wonderful?" Ma said over her shoulder.

"Yes! I'll learn how to read books and recite my baby C's!" Annie exclaimed.

"You mean your ABC's, silly," Drew corrected her with a laugh.

When they reached the schoolhouse, Drew leapt out of the buggy and tethered Lightning to a hitching post. Ma covered her basket with a wool scarf and started toward the door. "I'd better dash inside so these cookies don't become soaked. Logan and Tess, please bring Annie in with you," she called out.

"But I don't want Mrs. Wigglesworth to get wet!" Annie complained.

Logan pulled his Wonder Walkers out of their gunnysack. "Here, Annie. You can carry her in this," he said, handing her the sack.

"Thank you, Lolo! But what are those shiny things you're holding?" asked Annie.

"They are my latest and greatest

invention. Allow me to demonstrate how they work!"

Logan set the Wonder Walkers on the ground and stepped onto them. He grabbed the long straps and stomped through the wet, mucky grass. "You see? With Wonder Walkers, your shoes will never get muddy. The Wonders Walkers do!"

"What a clever idea!" said Tess.

Logan stepped off the Wonder Walkers and left them on the grass outside the door. They could stay there until recess.

Inside, everyone was already seated. Ma stood next to Miss Ashley, holding her basket of cookies. Logan shook the rain off and hurried to his desk.

"We have a visitor today," said Miss Ashley to the class. "Mrs. Pryce brought a special treat to welcome Wally to our community!"

In front of Logan, Wally slouched down as though he wanted to be invisible.

"But it's shortbread cookies. My ma makes the best ones in town!" Logan whispered to Wally.

"Really?" Wally sat up straight. He sounded happy all of a sudden.

Logan nodded to himself. Maybe Ma's plan was working!

"Mrs. Pryce will come around with her basket of cookies. Just one per person, please," Miss Ashley instructed.

Ma walked over to Wally's desk. "Welcome to Maple Ridge, Wally! You should choose the first cookie, since you're the guest of honor."

Wally reached into the basket
and took one of the larger cookies.

"Thank you, Mrs. Pryce," he said in a quiet voice.

"You're very welcome, Wally. I really hope you enjoy it."

But Wally didn't eat the cookie. Instead, he pulled a handkerchief out of his pocket, wrapped the cookie, and put it away.

Ma looked puzzled. So did Miss Ashley. So did everyone else.

Miss Ashley gave a little cough. "Yes, well . . . it's fine to save it for later if you're not hungry, Wally."

Wally blushed and stared out the window.

"What kind of weird kid doesn't like cookies?" Logan heard someone say.

"*Ann Elizabeth Pryce!*"

Logan whipped around. Ma was rushing across the room toward Annie.

Logan gasped. Annie was stomping around on his Wonder Walkers! She must have brought them inside.

"Where did you get those strange-looking things?" Ma demanded.

"They're Lolo's Under Walkers. Don't they make me look so very tall?

Like I'm six years old or maybe even twelve?" Annie said eagerly.

All eyes were on Logan. Anthony gave him a sympathetic smile. Logan rested his head on his hands.

Today was not quite a good day, after all.

CHAPTER 7

•THE MISSING BOOK•

At the end of the day, Miss Ashley told the students to choose their new library books for the week.

"To be fair, I'm starting a lottery system. I wrote down all your names on scrap paper and put them in this bonnet. When I say your name, you may go to the shelf and select your book," Miss Ashley explained.

"Please pick my name. Please pick my name," Tess murmured under her breath.

Miss Ashley held up a scrap of paper. "Tess Pryce!" she called out.

Beaming, Tess jumped to her feet and half ran to the library shelves.

She stopped in front of the B books and trailed her fingers across the spines. "*Birds of North America.* Where is *Birds of North America?* Wait, it's not here!" she cried out.

Miss Ashley frowned. "Hmm . . . did someone take it out last week?"

"*He* did!" Greta and Nellie both pointed to Wally.

Wally mumbled something.

"I'm sorry, Wally. What did you say?" asked Miss Ashley.

"I said I returned it to the shelf," Wally repeated. "First thing this morning. I put it back next to *The Blue Fairy Book*."

Tess scanned the shelves again. "No, it's definitely not here!"

"I'm sure there's a good explanation. Perhaps it ended up in the wrong place. Tess, is there another book you'd like to select?" asked Miss Ashley.

"No, ma'am. I've been waiting all week for this one," Tess said miserably.

"Well, then. I'll do another search for it later. In the meantime, let's continue with the lottery. It's nearly time to go home," Miss Ashley told the class.

Outside, everyone talked about Wally.

"I bet he stole the book," Lenny said snidely.

"He's a thief!" Greta agreed.

"A thief who won't eat cookies," Nellie added.

Drew and Tess got caught up in the discussion too. The only students who weren't saying mean things about Wally were Logan and Anthony . . . and Wally himself.

Logan and Anthony left the
schoolyard and started for home.
The rain had stopped, and the sun
was trying to peek through the
clouds. Logan carried his mud-

covered Wonder Walkers in one hand and his lunch pail in the other. He didn't have his gunnysack for carrying, since he had given that to Annie this morning.

Wally walked about thirty feet ahead of them, his shoulders slumped low.

"Do you think Wally stole the bird book?" Anthony asked Logan in a low voice.

"No," Logan replied as he stepped over a puddle. "Maybe we should find out for sure, though."

"How?"

"Why don't we follow him?" Logan suggested.

"You mean right now?"

"I mean right now."

"I promised Mama I'd clean out the barn. Maybe we could follow him tomorrow?"

"Or maybe I'll follow him on my own right now, and we can follow him again tomorrow."

The two friends said good-bye

and parted by the Pritchetts' apple orchard. Logan trailed after Wally, trying to be as quiet as possible.

Wally cut

through the apple orchard, and Logan stayed out of sight. Wally picked up his speed as he neared a patch of dense woods. Logan tried to keep up.

Where was Wally going? Was he on a spy mission?

Once in the woods, Wally paused and reached into his bag for something.

Logan slipped behind a tree, feeling like a spy himself. He tried to see what was in Wally's bag.

Could it be the bird book? he wondered.

CHAPTER 8

• FOR THE BIRDS •

Wally pulled something out of his bag.

But it wasn't the *Birds of North America* book. It was the short-bread cookie from this morning!

Logan watched in surprise as Wally crumbled up the cookie and scattered it onto the ground. A dozen birds flitted down from high branches and pecked eagerly at the crumbs.

"There you go, little birdies," Wally said softly. "I'll bring you another treat as soon as I'm able."

The birds continued pecking and chirping. Wally backed up ever so slowly and hunkered down under a

nearby maple. He pulled his leather notebook out of his bag and spread it across his lap.

"Excuse me, hello," Logan said in a whisper, so as not to bother the birds.

Wally's head shot up. "Logan! What are you doing here?"

"I was on my way home, and I saw you here and . . ." Logan paused. "You must like birds."

"Never you mind," Wally mumbled.

"We have a robin that nests in our barn. I named her Roberta," Logan added.

Wally's eyes flickered with a sudden

interest. "Birds are my favorite thing in the whole world," he confessed.

"Really?"

"Really. Here, take a look!" Wally handed Logan his leather notebook. Logan flipped through the pages. The notebook was filled with bird drawings! Flying birds . . . resting birds . . . nesting birds . . .

"Did you draw these? They're mighty good!" said Logan.

Wally smiled shyly. "Thanks."

"Why don't you show these to everyone at school?"

"Because." Wally dropped his gaze. He took off his feathered hat and crumpled it in his hands. "I don't know how to make new friends. The other kids think I'm odd. And now they think I stole the *Birds of North*

America book. I didn't, but no one believes me."

Logan was silent for a long moment. "I believe you," he said finally.

Wally's face lit up. "You do?"

"Yes! What do you say we find it together?"

And just like that, the new friends began to plan how to solve the mystery of the missing book.

CHAPTER 9

• THE MUDDY CLUE •

The first part of the plan was for Logan and Wally to return to the schoolhouse and search for the book there.

Along the way, the two of them talked about themselves. Logan talked about his family and Skeeter and Anthony and the Fix-It Shop. Wally talked about how he and his ma had moved to Maple Ridge to take care of his grandma while his pa stayed behind in Chicago to work for the railroads.

Wally also talked about his search for a bird called the yellow-billed cuckoo. "That's why I run around a lot. I don't see it often, and

when I do, I chase after it."

Logan and Wally finally reached the schoolhouse. Miss Ashley was inside, wiping down the blackboard. The other students had all gone home.

"Why, what are you boys doing here?" she asked curiously.

"We're detectives, and we're searching for the missing book!" replied Logan.

"Oh, right," said Miss Ashley, nodding. "The *Birds of North America*. I was just about to do another search for it. But you two go ahead.

I need to finish up with the blackboard and then mop the floor. The rain this morning made for a lot of muddy shoe prints."

Logan and Wally went over to the library shelves. They inspected each book carefully, one by one.

The bird book was not there.

Then Logan noticed something. Lots of muddy shoe prints covered the wooden floor, like Miss Ashley said. But there were some prints in front of the library shelves that weren't from shoes.

They were perfectly round—like tin cans.

"I know who took the book!" Logan announced.

CHAPTER 10

⊙ MYSTERY SOLVED! ⊙

The Pryce house was peaceful and still when Logan and Wally walked in. Tess and Ma were busy peeling potatoes in the kitchen. Skeeter was napping in front of the cookstove. Yesterday's laundry was drying on lines that stretched across the ceiling.

Logan set down his lunch pail

and Wonder Walkers. "Hi, Ma. Hi, Tess."

Tess pointed to Wally. "What is *he* doing here?"

"*Teresa Alice Pryce!* That is not how we welcome guests into our home," Ma scolded her. She turned to Wally with a friendly smile. "It's very nice to see you again, Wally."

Wally took off his hat. "Thank you, Mrs. Pryce."

"Where is Annie?" asked Logan.

"She's playing up in her room," replied Ma. "Why?"

Logan didn't answer. He raced out of the kitchen and up the stairs.

Wally followed
Logan. Ma and
Tess followed
Wally.

The four of
them found

Annie sitting on her bed, legs crisscross. She was wearing an old pair of glasses with the lenses missing and one of Ma's shawls. Mrs. Wigglesworth and a stack of three books were beside her.

"Annie! Here you are!" Logan said breathlessly.

Annie held her finger to her lips. "*Shhh*. Mrs. Wigglesworth and I are in the middle of school."

"School?" Wally repeated.

Annie turned to her doll. "Today is Libaby Day, Mrs. Wigglesworth. You may choose a book to read!"

Logan peered at the books on the bed. *Webster's Dictionary. A Wonder-Book for Girls and Boys.* Annie must have gotten them from the shelf downstairs.

The third book was *Birds of North America*.

"Is that what I think it is?" Tess exclaimed.

"Annie, where did you get the bird book?" Logan asked his little sister.

"Mrs. Wigglesworth wanted to learn about birds. So I brought it home for her from the *other* school," replied Annie.

"You mean the Maple Ridge School?" Ma chimed in.

Annie nodded. "Yes, Ma! I put it in Lolo's Under Walkers sack so it wouldn't get all wet and rainy."

Ma perched on the edge of the bed and hugged Annie. "Sweetheart, you know we mustn't ever take other people's things without asking first."

"I borrowed it from the libaby

just like the other kids," Annie said. "I'm sorry, Ma!"

"No, Wally. I should be sorry," Tess spoke up. "I believed Greta and the others when they said you were a thief. Will you forgive me? Can we be friends?"

She held out her hand. Wally shook it with a happy smile.

"All I can say is, thank *goodness* Annie took the Wonder Walkers without asking first," Wally pointed out.

"What do you mean, Wally?" Ma asked, surprised.

"Otherwise, she would never have left round prints in front of the library shelves. And Logan and I never would have solved the mystery!" replied Wally.

Everyone laughed.

Ma invited Wally to stay for supper, and Wally said yes. As they headed downstairs, Logan thought about how it was important not to judge a book by its cover. Wally had seemed like a lot of things at first:

an odd duck, a spy, even a thief. Logan and Tess had come to see that Wally was just a nice boy who loved birds. And starting tomorrow, they would help the other kids at school see that too!

TALES FROM MAPLE RIDGE

Find excerpts, activities, and more at
TalesfromMapleRidge.com!